Sword of Gold:
Heir to the Throne

JANE MYHRA

DEDICATION

This novel is dedicated to all who dream
and all who live their dream.

CONTENTS

ACKNOWLEDGMENTS

Editing, Proofreading ……... Terri Ellen Myhra

Comments, Poem …….......... Terri Ellen Myhra

Maps …............................ Alexander Christjohn

INTRODUCTION

BY TERRI ELLEN MYHRA

It is my great honor to present to you Jane's second novel in the *Sword of Gold* series, *Heir to the Throne*. I only hope that you find it as entrancing as I do with my sister's kaleidoscope of twists and turns that is inherent in what she does so well. Here is her magical story of kings and castles, a tale that embodies her gift with literature and everything she writes. Immerse yourself into a story that Jane weaves so well, one that has been spun so finely into gold.

CHAPTER 1

The Rightful King

BY JANE MYHRA

For as far back as time remembered, the island of Farway had been a peaceful kingdom. There was no famine; there were no wars, only contented people living in harmony with each other. The land was ruled by King Anthony who wanted his people to prosper and be happy.

King Anthony resided in a magnificent castle high above the city of Farway on the eastern coast of the island. The tall, white walls of the structure could be seen halfway across the flat lands that led to the Cinaria Mountain Range running through the center of the kingdom.

When King Anthony died, the crown passed from parent to sibling, as had been the custom for many generations. The king's eldest son, Prince Anthony, became King Anthony II, and all seemed right with the world.

Only one person, the king's second son, Prince William, was not pleased, for he believed he was better suited to rule the kingdom. He began secretively plotting to overthrow the new king and take control of the throne.

Meanwhile, King Anthony II mourned the passing of his beloved father and quietly celebrated being crowned the new king of Farway. His entire family and several loyal subjects were invited to a banquet held one week after his crowning. Sitting in his chambers, the new king opened the note that revealed that his brother was too ill to attend.

"I did not expect William to accept my invitation. He rarely frequents official events. I only wish he would allow his son, Wallace, to attend the banquet," the king said, frowning as he handed the letter to his son Robert, who served as his adviser.

"I do not think Uncle William is happy that you were crowned king," Robert replied.

"It is my destiny. I am the eldest son. I was raised to be the next ruler of Farway, and you will rule after I die," the king stated. He looked proudly at his only son, who at age nineteen already had the wisdom of a grown man.

"Hopefully that will be several decades from now!" Robert exclaimed. "I am too young to be king."

"My grandfather, King William III, took the throne when he was only eighteen, and he was considered this country's greatest ruler."

"I believe I still have a lot to learn before being allowed to rule a kingdom."

The king laughed, realizing that his son was a lot like him. Not only was he tall with the same dark brown hair, but he also was quite modest.

"Right now, you need to focus on your new wife," the king stated. "I must say I was quite pleased when you chose to marry Lady Carissa."

"It was an easy choice. I love her."

"Will she be at the celebration?"

"She hopes to return in time to attend the banquet."

****

Wallace whipped his horse into a gallop as he left his family's estate near Myornia. He could still hear his father's words ringing through his ears: "You know what I expect you to do! I am depending on you!" His head hurt when he thought about what his father expected. How could he betray his closest friend, his cousin who was almost like a brother to him?

Wallace stopped at the crossroads, rethinking his decision to leave the safety of his home without an escort. Under his brown cloak he wore the light armor of a soldier. It only took a moment for him to signal his horse to resume its gallop. It was a long ride to the forest where he hoped to find some answers.

By traveling steady throughout the night, Wallace reached the forest at daybreak. He dismounted near a stream and let his horse drink before he knelt to splash water on his face.

"Are you looking for me?" a voice spoke from a nearby grove of trees.

"Liam?" Wallace rose to his feet. A tall, black-haired man came slowly towards him. The dark-skinned man wore the plain clothes of the mountain people, but he walked like a nobleman with his dark brown eyes focused on some distant destination.

"You seem troubled, my friend," the stranger spoke.

"I am torn between duty to my friend and orders from my father," Wallace admitted. "I do not know where my allegiance lies."

"Your allegiance should be to yourself and yourself alone," Liam stated. He put a comforting hand on the young man's shoulder. "What is in your heart?"

"Nothing. It is empty."

"Come, sit down. I will make a fire and we will talk."

"I do not think there is a solution this time. I cannot betray my father!"

"There is always a solution," Liam said. He led Wallace to a clear spot near a big tree and motioned for him to sit on the ground.

"I must be back by noon tomorrow," Wallace said, watching his friend gather twigs to start a fire.

"You will be back, and you will know what to do."

Liam was right – Wallace left in an hour. He arrived home in time to see his father's soldiers preparing to leave. "I thought we were leaving tomorrow," he commented to his father, who was preparing to mount a horse.

"I changed my mind. We are leaving now," William replied. "Where have you been?"

"I was visiting a friend."

"Were you looking for a final kiss from a fair maiden before the battle?"

"Something like that, father." Wallace fidgeted, trying to look embarrassed.

"Good for you, son!" William slapped the young man's back. "Get a fresh horse for the prince!" He bellowed the order to his servants. When everyone was mounted, William turned again to his son. "Are you ready for this?"

"Yes, father."

Smiling proudly, William lifted a hand, then dropped it, signaling for his soldiers to depart. Wallace rode at his father's side as they headed for Farway Castle.

****

The crowd stood as King Anthony II entered the grand hall and offered a toast to begin the banquet. "Long live the kingdom of Farway!"

"Long live King Anthony!" the crowd replied. As soon as the king was served, the meal began.

Two hours later, the king and his twenty closest confidants gathered in the outer hall for a more private celebration. "Tonight, we are festive, but tomorrow the work begins," the king stated. "So, my friends, drink up and enjoy!"

"Too much celebrating can make one soft," Robert replied when he had a chance to talk privately to his father.

"You are like me, my son," the king laughed. "Instead of attending this party, I would rather be reading or practicing my swordsmanship."

"That is what will make you a good ruler, father."

Suddenly there was a loud bang. The main door flew open and hundreds of soldiers ran into the room and began slashing their swords at the crowd. The king's guards retaliated, but there were too many attackers.

"What is the meaning of this?" King Anthony II asked as he came face to face with his brother William.

"The crown is mine!" William said as he slashed his sword into his brother's chest. He pulled his bloody sword out of the king's dead body and held it high for all to see. "Long live King William IV!"

"Wallace?" Robert said as he faced the sword held by his cousin.

"Forgive me, Robbie," Wallace said as he pointed his sword at his cousin. "I have no choice. It is your life or mine."

"You always have a choice," Robert stated calmly.

"Now I will stab you and you will die," Wallace whispered as their eyes met. "You will die quickly because you are my friend."

The last thing Robert felt was the blade piercing his chest. He dropped to the floor next to his father.

William nodded his approval as he watched the crown prince fall, then beckoned Wallace to follow him to the throne room. His son had proven his loyalty.

"Now we celebrate!" William stated proudly.

With all the intended victims lying dead and dying, the new king and his soldiers left the room, leaving the mess for the servants to clean up in the morning.

No one noticed as another man entered the room, stepping over bodies until he reached Prince Robert and King Anthony II. He bent down and gently picked up one of the bodies. Then he left as swiftly as he had come.

****

Early the next afternoon, two riders stopped on a hilltop near Farway Castle. They watched solemnly as each body was carried to a mass burial site outside the castle grounds.

"That is no way to treat royalty," one of the soldiers stated.

"That is no way to treat anyone," the lead soldier replied. He dismounted, removed his helmet and knelt to honor the dead. The other soldier joined him.

"I should have been here to defend our king," the lead soldier said as they both stood up and remounted their horses.

"Do not blame yourself, Donovon. You were following the king's orders by escorting the princess. If you had been here, you would also be dead."

"I know. But it does not ease the guilt."

They were silent for several minutes before the other soldier asked, "Now what?"

"I refuse to serve a murderous king, so it looks like we are outcasts. I assume you agree, Nathan," Donovon waited for the other soldier to nod. "Our duty is to the princess. She will need our protection from King William. I am sure he has ordered her to be killed."

"The princess? She has no claim to this throne!"

"She is the wife of our dearly departed Prince Robert. That alone makes her a threat to William."

"Look, a rider is approaching!"

Donovon watched as a horse galloped toward them. He immediately recognized one of his own men, though he was not wearing armor. "Report!" he commanded.

"The king and his entire family are dead. William has claimed the throne!" the rider announced as he stopped his mount next to the other soldiers. "The new king has ordered the execution of anyone who remains loyal to King Anthony!"

"Did they mention Princess Carissa?" Nathan asked.

"Yes, William has ordered her killed, but no soldiers have been assigned the task," the rider answered.

"That is strange," Donovon stated. "It explains why we were able to get here without any trouble. Thank you, Winston."

"There is more," the messenger said. "I do not have it confirmed, but one of the servants told me that Prince Robert was not among the dead."

"How can that be?" Nathan asked. "We know he was at the scene."

"This servant told me that another was wearing his cloak and medallion," Winston stated. "Only someone who knew him well would have known the difference."

"It is but a rumor," Donovon spoke. "We must not repeat a word of this until it is confirmed."

"The princess will be pleased!" Nathan exclaimed.

"The princess will not be told," Donovon ordered. "If this is a rumor, we cannot give her false hope."

"If Robert is not dead, where is he?" Nathan asked. "How did he escape the massacre?"

"We will find our answers in the mountains," Donovon said as he turned his horse away from the castle.

"This news will be hard to keep from the princess," Nathan mumbled as he followed.

"Winston," Donovon called over his shoulder. "You remain here and mingle with the castle guards. There may be more secrets to uncover!"

"Yes, sir!" Winston answered as he watched the two soldiers gallop away. Then he slowly made his way back to the castle.

****

It was starting to rain as the lone horseman approached a clearing in the woods that led to the Cinaria Mountains. He stopped briefly to check the status of the body draped behind his saddle. The prince was still breathing.

"Lianna!" he called into the darkness of the forest. "Lianna, are you here?"

A tall, slender woman walked slowly toward him. "Yes, Liam, I received your message to meet you here. What is so urgent?" Then she noticed the injured man. "Who is he?"

Liam lifted the limp body gently onto the ground and signaled for the woman to approach. "He is near death."

"Then you need a priest, not me," Lianna stated coldly as she looked down at the injured man.

"We cannot let him die!" Liam shouted. "You must save him!"

"No," the woman murmured to herself. "No."

"As your brother, I beg you to save this man's life!"

She looked into Liam's dark eyes and saw his determination. At that moment, she needed no further explanation. Lianna knelt beside the injured man and placed her hands over the wound on his chest. Her eyes closed and her face turned white as she transferred her life force to the injured body. After several minutes, she collapsed over the body.

Liam gently picked up his sister, set her against a tree and covered her with his own cloak. He stroked her long, black hair and gently kissed her on the forehead before returning to the injured man who seemed to be breathing better after being touched by Lianna.

"We will take him to the cave," Liam said, though no one heard his words. He carefully laid the injured man across the back of his horse, then mounted and rode towards the highest mountain, leaving Lianna alone in the clearing.

The sun was starting to set when they reached the cave. Liam carried the prince through several tunnels and cautiously positioned him on a pile of furs in the largest cavern. Then he began to make a fire, for the cave was damp and cold. Lianna reached the cave as the sun began to rise. She looked weak and tired.

"I am sorry, Lianna, but we had no choice," Liam told her. "We needed to save Prince Robert."

"The crown prince? How was he injured?"

"Prince William has killed the king and claimed the throne. Saving the prince is our only hope to reclaim the kingdom." He watched as his sister turned away and began to swoon, as if in a trance.

"I foresee many years of darkness," Lianna said softly. "We may have saved Prince Robert, but he will never reclaim the throne."

"That is not what I want to hear!"

"I only tell you what I foresee. I do not control the future."

"But will he live?"

"He has made it this far, so he should live. The cave will help heal him."

"Without your help, Lianna, he never would have made it to this cave."

"You do know that every time I help someone, I grow weaker and my life becomes shorter."

"I would not have asked you if it was not important."

"Yes, I know."

"What else do you foresee?"

"It comes when it comes. I cannot force the future to reveal itself."

"Then you have told me everything?"

"I always tell you everything, Liam."

CHAPTER 2

Beyond the Mountains

King William was furious. His eyes turned red and he growled like a cornered bear. "I ordered the princess killed!" he yelled. "How did she escape?"

"We could not find her, Your Majesty," the soldier reported. "She was not on the roadway leading to the castle. We searched the countryside, to no avail." The soldier fidgeted and did not look directly into the eyes of his new ruler. The king read the soldier's uneasiness and knew immediately that the report was a lie. The soldier had not followed orders.

"I do not want excuses – I want her found! I want her dead – dead like the others! Dead like you will be!" the king bellowed. He waved his hand and two guards escorted the soldier from the throne room.

"Father," Prince Wallace spoke softly, so only his father could hear. "She is no threat to your crown."

"Princess Carissa is a member of my brother's family."

"I cannot believe you intend to murder a woman!"

"It is not murder. I am securing my throne. Someday you will understand how other family members become your biggest threat."

"I do not want Carissa killed."

"And why is that?" The king quickly became calmer at this new development.

"I will marry her."

"Now that surprises me!" the king laughed. "You are actually thinking of marriage? I can hardly get you to talk to a woman, much less marry one!"

"I would marry Carissa," Wallace said. "I love her."

"So be it," the king stated. "But first we must find her."

"Do not send out the soldiers," the young man offered. "Let me find her."

"Very well. I will give you four days, then I will send out every soldier I can spare. I must warn you, though, they have orders to kill her."

"I will find her!"

Wallace left the throne room knowing he had bought his friends some extra time by claiming to be in love with Carissa. But it was not a total lie, for he did love her as a brother would love a sister. His feelings for her were the same as his feelings for Robert.

He leaned against a wall and closed his eyes as he whispered a prayer for the safety of his friends. At this moment, Wallace felt closer to them than to his own father, whom he had come to realize was a murderous tyrant. He could feel no love for such an evil soul.

****

Lianna gently changed the cold cloth on the injured man's forehead, humming softly as she worked. The used cloth did not feel warm, which was a good sign. She smiled. The soothing aura of the cave was beginning to heal him. His eyes opened.

"Good morning," Lianna said soothingly. "Are you feeling better?"

The man looked confused as his eyes scanned the large room. Then he murmured, "You are beautiful. Is this heaven? Are you an angel?"

"No, you are not dead," Lianna replied. "We brought you here so you could heal."

"I was killed. Wallace betrayed me!" The patient tried to sit up, but Lianna held him down. He was too weak to resist.

"You were severely injured. As for the other details, you will need to ask my brother, Liam."

"Is my father dead?"

"Yes, everyone else was killed," Lianna said sadly.

The man's eyes closed for a moment and tears began to flow down the sides of his cheeks. "Did you say everyone was killed? Why was I spared?"

"You need to talk to Liam. He will be here soon."

"I should also be dead!"

"Liam will explain everything when he arrives," Lianna tried to soothe the prince.

"Who is this Liam?"

"Liam is my brother. He brought you here after the massacre. He said you were the only survivor."

"Carissa! They could not have killed Carissa! She was not there!"

"I do not know about Carissa. Who is she?"

Instead of being filled with despair, the man's eyes began to reveal a glimmer of hope. "She is my wife. I must find her!"

"You are too weak. You need to rest. Must I restrain you?

The man stared into her dark eyes. "You would not tie me down! Do you know who I am?"

"You are my patient. Your health is my only concern. Drink this." Lianna held a cup to his lips until he drank the warm liquid. "Now relax."

"What did you put in that water?" the patient asked as his eyes began to close.

"Merely medicine to help you sleep. You need three more days of rest."

"I could have you ... punished for ... poisoning me," Robert mumbled as he fought the drowsiness.

"You, my dear prince, are in no condition to threaten me," Lianna smiled as she watched her patient slip into slumber.

"How is he?" Liam asked, approaching his sister.

"Oh, you have returned," Lianna stood up and faced her brother. "He awoke, but I convinced him to go back to sleep."

"With one of your concoctions, I am sure," Liam laughed. "How long will he sleep?"

"Several hours," she replied. "Several hours."

"We have another problem, Lianna." Liam took her arm and led her away from the patient. "King William has ordered the entire royal family killed."

"Why would that concern us?"

"We must keep Prince Robert hidden from everyone. He needs to remain with us."

"But, Liam, you know he cannot stay here for more than a few days without being affected by the cave's magic."

"We will need to take that chance or find another place to hide him," Liam stated. "I believe he is safest here."

"The prince can stay in the cave as long as he is healing. I would not want to risk any long-term exposure."

"The cave might have no effect on him," Liam said.

"We cannot take that chance."

****

King William was determined to rule the isle of Farway with an iron hand, and he was ruthless in his discipline. His soldiers rode throughout the land searching for those who were disloyal to the crown. Despite the king's efforts, the unrest increased, as did the arrests and executions. The kingdom appeared to be on the verge of an uprising.

In the sanctuary of the well-fortified castle, King William sat regally on his gold-plated throne surrounded by guards, servants and his most trusted advisers. This was his designated hour for commoner comments, but no visitors came, which annoyed the king. After waiting for half an hour, he angrily stood up and strode out of the throne room followed by his lead adviser, Counselor Saffen.

"I give the peasants a chance to voice their opinions and they shun me!" King William shouted as he entered his office area. "I am their ruler!"

"Many are still loyal to your brother," Saffen calmly stated.

"My brother is dead! His entire family is dead!"

"The people believe you had them murdered and therefore they do not accept you as their king," Saffen said.

"There is nothing they can do about it!"

"Your Majesty, I worry that the people might revolt and attempt to dethrone you."

"Let them try! They have no resources and their strongest young men are my soldiers! I hold all the power! They cannot defeat me!"

"Please, Your Majesty, calm down. There is no reason to get so upset." With his back to the king, Saffen poured a large cup of brandy, added a few drops of his own secret formula, and handed it to the king. "Eventually, the people will have no choice but to accept you as their monarch."

King William sank into a nearby chair and began to sip the brandy. Somehow, Saffen always made him feel better. Perhaps it was the brandy? After a few minutes the king asked, "Are there any pressing matters today?"

"None, Your Majesty."

"Then I wish to talk to Captain Worth," the king stated.

"Yes, Your Majesty!" Saffen bowed several times as he backed out of the room. He returned with a soldier who was older and broader than most. His short beard had a twinge of gray and his eyes were narrow and black.

"Captain Worth, have you located Princess Carissa?"

"No, Your Majesty. I was told to wait four days," the soldier said as he bowed deeply. "Have I disappointed my king in some way? Was that not an official order, Your Majesty?"

"Never think you are a disappointment! You are my best warrior! My friend, without you I would not wear this crown!"

"I have always followed your commands, Your Majesty." The soldier bowed again.

"I wish you to locate this princess and bring her to me. Take only a handful of your most trusted men. I do not want her harmed!"

"Yes, Your Majesty!" The soldier bowed twice before leaving the room.

"Saffen!" the king called, and the counselor appeared.

"Yes, Your Majesty!"

"Did you overhear that conversation?"

"No, Your Majesty."

"I know you heard everything, Saffen – you always do." The king calmly gulped down the last swallow of brandy.

"Your orders to Captain Worth confused me a bit, sire, especially since I had previously heard you order the soldiers to kill Princess Carissa." Saffen said as he quickly took away the empty cup.

"Yes, the change also came as a surprise to me!" the king laughed. "It seems my son actually wants to marry this princess. Imagine that – my son married! Far be it for me to stand in the way!"

"That is great news, Your Majesty!"

"Just think, Saffen, I may actually become a grandfather with heirs to carry on my name!"

"You told me you intend to live forever."

"Yes, I will," the king smiled. "I have no choice. I certainly cannot leave this kingdom to that spineless child of mine. He would have no clue how to rule! He spent too much time with his mother. Things will be different with my grandson!"

****

The two horsemen stopped outside the cave and waited to be invited inside. Liam had heard them arrive and hurried to the cave's entrance.

"Wallace!" Liam said. "I did not expect you so soon!"

"Greetings, Liam!" Wallace dismounted. "This is my friend Daniel. How is Robert?"

"He is alive and almost ready to leave the cave," Liam stated. "Most of the time he sleeps, so I have not explained what happened. That might be best coming from you."

"He probably will not believe that I never meant to kill him." Wallace hesitated before entering the cave.

"You two are like brothers," Liam stated. "Just explain the circumstances."

"I should not have come!" Wallace groaned. "I will only make matters worse."

"You care about him, Wallace. Just say that." Liam led his friend into the cave, through several tunnels toward the large cavern.

"I can feel the magic within these walls," Daniel said as he followed them.

"Some people are more sensitive to it than others. The aura gives mystic powers to a choice few, but to some it can have an adverse effect," Liam remarked. "Perhaps you should wait outside."

"We will not stay long," Wallace said as he gave Daniel a signal to stay with him.

Robert was awake as they entered the large cavern. He reached for a sword, only to find no weapon near him. Wallace stopped at the entrance as Liam hurried towards the patient who was struggling to sit up.

"Stay calm and hear him out!" Liam ordered. He gently placed his hands onto Robert's shoulders and held him still. "He means you no harm!"

"You murdered my family! You tried to murder me!" Robert shouted at Wallace. "I trusted you!"

At that moment, Lianna stepped into the room from the opposite direction. She stopped abruptly when she saw Wallace.

"Actually, he saved you," Liam stated. "Without his help you would have died."

"No! He attacked me and left me for dead!"

"His sword was not aimed at your heart," Liam explained. "He only injured you. The sedative on the sword tip made you appear dead. I was there for the sole purpose of bringing you here immediately."

Robert still looked doubtful. He looked at Liam, then at Wallace.

"It is true," Wallace spoke. "I did not want you to die. You are like a brother to me!" He walked slowly toward Robert. "I have never killed anyone, but my father believes I killed you." He held out a hand to his cousin and Robert grasped it. Then they embraced.

Seeing that there was no longer any danger to her patient, Lianna slowly backed out of the room.

"I am worried about Carissa," Robert told his cousin.

"You know I will do everything to protect her," Wallace promised.

"He needs to rest now," Liam said after the two had talked for several minutes.

Wallace and Daniel followed Liam to the cave exit.

"What now?" Wallace asked.

"We must keep his existence a secret for a long time, even after he is totally recovered," Liam replied. "His life will be in danger until he is surrounded by a strong army."

"I will be at his side when the time comes," Wallace said after he mounted his horse. "But for now, I must return to my father or he will become suspicious."

Liam nodded his approval and waved as the two rode away. Then he turned to find Lianna behind him.

"Are you sure we can trust both of them?" she asked.

"I have known Wallace for a long time, and he can be trusted. He is not like his father."

"That is good," Lianna said. "I feel he has some loyalty to the new king, but he may soon need to choose between his father and his friends. The more powerful King William becomes, the further away he will push his son. In the end there will be only one allegiance."

"I trust Wallace will make the right decision when that time comes," Liam stated.

Lianna started to walk away from the cave.

"Where are you going?" Liam asked.

"I need a few more herbs," his sister stated. "Keep an eye on the patient until I return."

When she neared a grove of trees, Lianna turned to see Liam re-enter the cave. Satisfied that she would not be followed, she quickened her pace and headed down the mountain slope into the thickness of the forest. Suddenly someone grabbed her.

"Wallace!" she exclaimed. "I knew you would wait for me!"

"Being away from you is more than I can bear!" Wallace said as he embraced and kissed her. "I wish I could stay with you forever!"

"We are together now, my love!"

****

Donovon helped Princess Carissa onto her horse. This was their third stop since they had reached the mountain path. "Are you sure we should continue?" he asked her. "You do not seem well today, and the trail is very rough." The paleness of her face worried him.

"I will be fine," Carissa stated. "I must see Robert!"

Donovon shot an angry look at Nathan, who had accompanied them on the journey. "This is why you should not have told her!" he snapped at Nathan.

"She needed to know the truth," the other soldier replied.

"I am glad Nathan told me, for I was sick with grief when I heard of the massacre." Carissa glared angrily at Donovon before she clicked her horse into a trot and continued up the mountainside. The men followed.

They eventually reached the cave where they found Liam waiting at the entrance. "Sir Donovon, what brings you here?" Liam did not seem surprised.

"Princess Carissa, this is Liam, known to some as Captain Liam," Donovon introduced the two. "The princess wishes to see her husband."

"How did you know to come here?" Liam asked.

The soldiers dismounted and Nathan helped the princess down from her saddle. The three followed Liam into the darkness of the cave. Donovon proceeded the princess, with Nathan in the rear.

"When I heard rumors that the prince was alive, I knew who was responsible," Donovon explained. "Did you forget that I have been to this cave many times?"

"Yes, you always come after being injured in battle," Liam acknowledged. "I believe you have been here on five occasions."

"And five times I almost died," Donovon stated. "I know the healing powers of this cave."

"I have heard that this place also has other powers," Nathan said. His eyes were filled with wonder as he looked around the main cavern with its smooth, gray walls, so unlike the rough rock found in the cave's tunnels.

"Robert!" Carissa exclaimed when she saw the prince. She rushed to his side and gathered him into her arms. "You are alive! Thank God!"

"Carissa!" the prince kissed his wife and embraced her. "I did not expect you to come here. I was afraid they had captured and killed you!"

"I am safe," she said. "Are you well?"

"He should be able to travel in about two days," stated Lianna, who had just arrived through the cavern's back entrance. "It will take several months for him to regain his full strength."

"I have a place where we can hide him," Donovon announced. "There is a fortress on the north side of the mountain range. He will be safe there."

"You and your friends can only remain in this cave a few hours. Then you must leave," Liam told Carissa. "Return in two days and Robert will be ready to travel." Then he turned to Donovon. "Do you have extra horses?"

"Yes, I will bring them. Will you be traveling with us?" Donovon asked.

"No, I have other things to do," Liam answered.

Lianna stood up. "We should leave them alone for a few minutes," she suggested. She led the others into a large hallway, leaving behind the prince and princess, who were passionately kissing.

Lianna signaled for the three men to sit on a rock ledge while she disappeared down another corridor to gather refreshments for them.

"Liam, I hope you realize we do not have enough soldiers to overthrow King William," Donovon reported. "The new king has control of the entire army. All that resisted were put to death. It will take years to rebuild a following for Prince Robert."

"Lianna foresaw that Robert will never be crowned king," Liam revealed. "She also said the kingdom will be split into thirds."

"Of course! That makes sense," Donovon exclaimed. "With the placement of the mountain range and Glover River, it will be easy to divide the island. King William probably will not waste his troops protecting the western lands, which hold no benefit for him. He will probably allow those regions to continue to be ruled and protected by their regents."

"We must be sure the regents are not loyal to King William," Liam warned.

"That should not be hard," Nathan stated. "King William is a tyrant. His subjects only obey him out of fear."

"True, but we must be sure the regents are loyal to us," Donovon remarked. "Are you acquainted with them, Liam?"

"Robert's second cousin, Prince Albert, is regent in Ashland, and a more distant cousin, Lord Howard, rules in the Glover region. Both would be loyal to the true heir," Liam said.

"But is there hope? Remember, your sister foresaw that Robert will never be crowned king," Donovon seemed greatly concerned. "Lianna's predictions are never wrong."

"We will worry about that when the time comes," Liam answered. "The main thing is to keep everyone safe until we are ready to return to Farway. We must secretly build our strength and remain united."

"How many months must we remain under King William's rule?" Nathan questioned.

"Months?" Liam remarked. "Your youth makes you far too anxious, Nathan. It may take many years for us to reunite this kingdom."

"I am behind you, Captain Liam," Donovon knelt, holding his gilded sword upwards.

"No, Sir Donovon, you will not follow me, for you are to lead," Liam spoke. Grabbing his arms, Liam lifted the soldier to his feet. "Lianna foresaw that the greatest warrior will lead us. There is none greater than you, Donovon."

"I am not up to the task. You have far more experience, Liam!" Donovon protested.

"You have been chosen," Liam said as he and Nathan knelt before Donovon.

CHAPTER 3

A Matter of Trust

King William sat on his throne sipping brandy as he waited for Captain Worth to finish his report.

"The princess cannot be found," the soldier was saying. "The last sighting was three weeks ago in Tector."

"You will continue the search," the king ordered.

"As you command, Your Majesty!" Worth saluted, then knelt before leaving the throne room.

"He will never find her," Saffen sneered as he moved closer to the king. "The traitors have her hidden in the mountains and that is a place our soldiers fear."

"Are you inferring that my soldiers are cowards?" the king bellowed.

"No, Your Majesty, I would never call your soldiers cowards!" Saffen retracted quickly. "They respect the magical powers of the mountains and are wise not to venture there."

"Perhaps, but we can find men to search the mountains, for the right price. In fact, I plan to make that your responsibility, Saffen!"

"I am honored that you trust me, Your Majesty! But am I not needed at your side? I could assign that task to another."

"So be it," the king agreed. "Just see that it is done!"

"Yes, Your Majesty!"

"We cannot rest until my brother's entire family is annihilated! Only then will the people accept me as their monarch!"

"Yes, Your Majesty!"

"You all may leave me now."

The king watched as the entire room was cleared. Then he turned to Saffen, who remained. "Was there something else?" the king asked.

"One matter of grave importance, Your Majesty. But I do not know if I am worthy to give it mention."

"That sounds rather ominous." The king sank back into his throne and closed his eyes. It had been a long, tiring day dealing with various matters of state and he did not want to hear any bad news.

"It is about your son." Saffen handed the king another brandy.

"Now what has he done?"

"I suspect he will betray you."

The king sat upright and glared in disbelief at Saffen. "How dare you accuse my son of treason! He has proven his loyalty! I saw him kill his beloved cousin! He would never betray me! He loves me!"

"As you love him." Saffen remained calm and spoke softly.

"I have no choice but to I love him. He is my son." The king became somewhat calmer. "What brings you to believe he will betray me?"

"I saw how he looked at you before he left here."

"And?"

"There was a glimmer of hatred, even jealousy in his eyes."

"Is that the only reason you suspect him?"

"Also, I believe he loves another, yet claimed he loves Carissa."

"You will keep these suspicions to yourself, Saffen."

"I only want you to be warned, Your Majesty. I want no harm to come to you!"

"I appreciate your concern, Saffen. I will talk to Wallace."

"Thank you, Your Majesty!" the adviser bowed deeply, then backed away.

Upon entering the hallway Saffen slammed his fist against the wall in anger. The encounter had not gone as he had planned. Perhaps he needed to increase the king's dosage of the secret concoction, he wondered. No, too much poison could kill the king too quickly. Saffen took a deep breath and began to plot his next accusation against the prince. It bothered him deeply that Wallace was the only person who stood between him and the king's trust, between him and total control of the kingdom.

****

"Come," Liam spoke. "I have something to show you." Wrapping his dark robe tighter over his shoulders, Liam led Donovon and Nathan into the smaller winding tunnels of the mountain cave. The two soldiers followed him down to the deepest, hidden areas, into a small cavern. They watched as Liam pulled a large chest out from behind a rock. He then took out two swords and handed one to each of them.

Donovon held the sword up to catch a small ray of light, which shimmered on the golden edges of the sword. "It is gold!" he exclaimed.

"These are special swords, specifically created to protect the rightful heirs to the Farway throne," Liam announced. "You two have been chosen to wield these swords and protect the royal family's lineage."

"I have always protected the royal family, as has Nathan," Donovon stated.

"You will need these swords in the days ahead," Liam said. "From this day forward, these swords will be passed down through the generations to forever protect the true heirs to the throne."

"Are they magical?" Nathan asked as he studied the blade of his new weapon.

"They have been in this cave for many years," Liam stated. "As a result, these swords may have powers even I do not understand."

"I have never seen such well-crafted swords." Donovon lightly brushed a finger along the sharp edge of the golden sword.

"You, Sir Donovon, will be the sword master, the one who will guide the others," Liam said. "Your sword will always be closest to the true heir to the throne."

"Does that mean I am assigned to Prince Robert?"

"Your swords will tell you who to protect. That is not for me to determine." Liam looked away as he made this statement, and his eyes were filled with sadness.

"Is something wrong?" Donovon asked.

"It may be several years before we see peace again," Liam said. "These swords will be our only chance to survive."

"Are there only two swords?" Nathan asked.

"There are four," Liam replied.

"Who holds the other two?" Donovon asked.

"That must remain a secret, even from me," Liam said.

"How can I be the sword master if I do not know the swordsmen?"

"It will all be revealed in time, Sir Donovon," Liam answered. "Now, Donovon, I have one more thing to discuss with you. Please meet me in town in two hours."

****

Lianna watched as Liam rode away. She knew he would be gone until it was time for their patient to leave. She turned and walked into the cave to find Wallace waiting for her.

"You said we would be alone, but the prince is still here," Wallace stated.

"Robert will sleep for several hours, trust me," Lianna smiled as she moved into his arms and kissed him. He returned her kiss and embraced her. "Wait!" She pulled away from him.

"What is wrong?" he asked.

"I have something to give you." She took his hand and led him to her private quarters. "It is here." She bent down to push a heavy stone set against the wall. Wallace moved her aside to easily move the stone himself. All he found was an empty hole in the wall.

"I need no gift from you, my love," he said.

"This is more than a gift and has nothing to do with our love," she stated. Lianna knelt, reached into the hole and pulled out a long, narrow bundle. She placed it at his feet. "Open it carefully," she warned.

Wallace unwrapped the clothes and was surprised by what he found. "It is a sword!" he exclaimed.

"A special sword," she whispered.

"It is beautiful!" Wallace held up the sword, which shimmered gold in the dim light of the small room.

"It is a specially-forged sword from a distant land. It will give you strength in battle."

"Why do you say it is more than a gift?" He expertly swung the sword to his left, then to his right. "What is this sword? It feels enchanted."

"The swords have been in this cave for many decades."

"Swords? There are more?"

"Four in total."

"Do they have special powers from being in the cave?"

"Perhaps, but I am not sure," Lianna spoke. "What I do know is that these swords will protect the members of the royal family, for they have been predestined to do so."

"Predestined? By whom?" Wallace carefully unsheathed his sword and replaced it with the new one. He turned back to face Lianna, only to find her swooning into a trance.

"I have foreseen it. Each sword will forever protect a potential heir to the Farway throne. Each sword bearer will know when their person is in danger so they can be there to protect them. Throughout the generations, gold swords will be passed to expert swordsmen to protect future heirs to the throne."

Wallace listened and began to realize the meaning of the gift.

"You gave a sword to me, Lianna. Does that mean I am to protect a future heir to the throne?"

"Yes, you have been chosen." She was slowly coming out of the trance.

"That means I am not an heir to the throne."

"Does that bother you?"

"No, but it slightly confuses me. I am the only nephew of King Anthony and the only son of the present king. Am I to protect Robert?"

"Donovon will protect Robert. I do not know who you will protect."

"How will I know?"

"You will know."

"Who will carry the other swords?"

"I do not yet know."

"You have so many responsibilities, Lianna." Wallace said. "Sometimes I wish you could leave this cave and never return. Perhaps then you could live a normal life and no longer have visions of the future. It is such a burden for you to bear!"

"Someone must bear the burden, especially in these times of turmoil."

"Come, my love, let me ease your worries and help you forget about the world's troubles for a while." He took her hand and kissed it. Then he gathered her into his arms.

****

Donovon met Liam in a small ale house in a nearby town, as planned.

"I see you did not bring your young friend today," Liam said. They sat at a table in a secluded corner.

"Nathan does not quite understand the importance of our strategy. He better serves us by standing guard outside of town."

"I agree. And where is Princess Carissa?"

"She is watched by my most trusted soldiers. I left Ivan in charge."

"The king's men are still searching for her. Are you sure this fortress is well hidden?"

"It is accessible only by water, then by rope ladders kept up high until needed. The fortress is hidden in the rockiest area of the mountain range. It was last used several hundred years ago."

"Your job is to protect the prince and princess at all costs."

"You know I will guard them with my life," Donovon vowed. "There is no question about that!"

"We do not know what the future holds, so we must be prepared for anything and everything," Liam warned.

"That is how I was trained as a soldier."

"Which is exactly why you were chosen to protect them."

"And what is your task, Liam?"

"I am not sure. I only know that it will become known to me. In the past, my job has been to protect my sister and the cave. That is why I am no longer a soldier."

"Lianna is important, for she is the one who foresees the future."

"She provides valuable information," Liam agreed. "We could not do this without her."

"Are you also able to see the future?"

"No, the cave does not give me that power."

"Then what power does it give you?"

"First and foremost, I am given the power to keep secrets," Liam stated. "More than that, I cannot tell you."

"With your negotiation skills, you would be the best person to visit Glover and Ashland."

"I will do the traveling, so you must protect the prince."
Liam stood up.

"Are we done here?"

"Yes, I will see you at the cave tomorrow."

"We will be there by mid-morning."

"See that you are not followed," Liam cautioned.

"Always!"

****

The streets below Farway Castle were busy as Saffen made his way to the designated meeting place. No one was in the abandoned stable when he arrived, so he waited impatiently in the dark until a dark-cloaked stranger slipped through the back door.

"Are you the king's messenger?" the newcomer asked in a gruff voice, with his bearded face mostly hidden by a hooded cloak. He moved in a circle around Saffen.

"Yes." Saffen handed a bag of gold to the stranger who grabbed it greedily. "The gold will triple when the job is done."

"Nice! What do you need me to do?"

"Kill Princess Carissa."

"It is done."

"And tell no one!"

The man nodded and began to leave. Near the door he turned and said, "My men and I will attend to this matter immediately, so expect me to return for the money within a week."

Saffen smiled as the stranger left. Yes, thieves were the right people to hire. They were willing to do anything – for a price. He laughed evilly to himself as he thought about his promise to increase the bounty. Yes, he would make sure they got what they deserved – not one of them would be left alive to brag about what they had done.

Saffen slipped into the marketplace, stopping briefly to purchase a few ingredients at a medicine booth before heading swiftly back to the castle. Winston followed at a safe distance.

****

Prince Robert and Princess Carissa watched as the first soldiers traversed the ropes leading to the fortress in the mountains.

"I am not strong enough to climb the ropes," the prince stated. "And I definitely will not allow the princess to make the climb."

"I have thought about that, Your Highness," Donovon replied. He pointed to the top of the steep cliff where a carriage was being lowered by several heavy ropes. "You and the princess will ride in style!"

"Thank you, Donovon," the prince smiled. "You have been quite accommodating to us on this trip."

"Only the best for our future king," Donovon bowed. He knew this statement went against what Lianna predicted, but for the moment he was the protector of this heir to the throne and that required him to believe it was true.

Donovon's hand gently touched the sword at his side, hidden by his long, blue cloak. With such a sword came obligations and a promise to defend this prince to the death. He took his job seriously and even rode in the carriage with the royal couple as they ascended to the top of the mountain. He had no intentions of letting Robert out of his sight until he was sure the prince was safe.

Once they were on solid ground again, Robert helped Carissa out of the carriage, being cautious not to let her long skirt get tangled in the hinges that held the door. Robert led his wife away from the cliff's edge, politely signaling for the soldiers to keep their distance. He would not let anyone else near the princess. Carissa gazed down at the boats in the lake far below them, but the prince only looked forward toward the fortress where they were expected to spend the next several months.

"How would we ever escape if we were attacked?" Carissa asked Donovon.

"No one will find us here and, if they attacked, they would not be successful. This is a highly fortified mountain," Donovon assured her.

"But what if we needed to escape?" the princess persisted.

"There are tunnels, but only a few know of them," Donovon whispered to only her.

"That makes me feel safer, Donovon, thank you."

"Come, Carissa, this is our new home," Robert called to her from a few steps away. He reached out to take her hand.

"For a while it is our home," she replied. "Until we return to Farway as king and queen." She smiled at Robert, for any place was home to her when she was with her beloved husband.

"Nathan will escort you to your quarters," Donovon announced. He turned back to the edge of the cliff and signaled for the boats to depart. They were scheduled to take the longest route back to Cinaria so as not to reveal the secret hideout.

Donovon's next job was to ensure that everything was in order. He checked in with the soldiers who had been assigned to protect the fortress before he allowed himself a brief visit with his wife and children who had arrived with the first soldiers. Later he would join the prince and princess, then remain close to them throughout their stay.

Carissa walked out onto the balcony of the new quarters she shared with Robert. "It is beautiful here," she sighed. "And I am so happy to be reunited with you."

"I thought I would never see you again," Robert said, coming up behind her and kissing her on the neck. "I cannot imagine ever loving you more than I do at this moment."

"Our love will continue to grow now that we are together."

"Hopefully forever!"

****

Everything was calm and the mountains outside were strangely quiet. When Liam stepped outside the cave, he sensed that something was wrong. He felt a strange tingling in his stomach which had always warned him of impending danger. He quickly climbed above the cave entrance where he had a better view of all the trails cascading toward the mountains. As he focused his eyes, he could see a group of about twenty riders on the north trail. They were dressed like thieves, but what would thieves be doing in the mountains where there was nothing to steal?

Lianna felt her brother's concern and exited the cave. Yes, something was wrong, but she did not know what it was. She felt a sense of restlessness and impending danger. She searched relentlessly for images of the future and found only emptiness. Why were the answers unattainable? What did this all mean?

The thief Drabo led his men up the mountain trail with confidence. From the townspeople he had tortured he learned that a caravan had gone up this trail about a week ago. These days, no one entered the mountain range unless they wanted to hide something or someone. The mountains were too dangerous for the casual traveler.

"Onward! Faster!" he encouraged his men. Their main motive was the award that awaited them at the end of this journey, so they did not need his encouragement, but it was Drabo's way of reminding them who was in charge.

"Look!" one of the men shouted. "What is that?"

Drabo stopped his horse at the sight of a huge cloud rumbling down the trail toward them. It grew larger, darker and louder as it neared. Trees were breaking as the cloud collided with the sides of the trail. A strange smell filled the air and the rumbling became louder than thunder. It only took a moment for Drabo to turn his horse and shout, "Run!" But it was too late. The cloud overtook the riders and sent the men and horses flying down the mountainside. Their screams were deafened by the roar of the cloud.

Liam returned to the cave, exhausted.

"What happened?" Lianna asked. Her eyes were filled with fear.

"Do not worry, Lianna, they are safe," was all he said. He took her hand and led her back into the cave.

CHAPTER 4

Legacies and Conspiracies

The king watched as his son approached the throne and bowed before him. "I wish to talk to my son alone," the king ordered, and everyone else immediately left the room.

"Father," Wallace said, rising. But he stayed below the three steps that led up to the throne. "I have returned empty-handed."

"That is most unfortunate," the king answered. "I was so looking forward to your wedding. Perhaps we should find another bride?"

"I am sorry, father, but I love only her."

"When you refer to her, do you mean Carissa?"

"Yes." Wallace hesitated and took a deep breath. "My only love is Princess Carissa."

"You lie!" the king shouted angrily, rising from the throne. "She is not the one you love!"

"Father, who has put this doubt in your mind?" Wallace worked hard to appear calm. "I would never deceive the father that I love! Who has turned you against me? There must be a considerable amount of hate in that person's heart."

The king sat back in his throne, suddenly feeling a bit dizzy. As he gazed into his son's eyes, his voice became softer. "I am sorry, my son, I forget there is only love in your heart for me. Please, I offer my condolences on the loss of your one true love. Judging by your reaction to my accusations, she most certainly means everything to you."

"Yes, father, I am very much in love."

"I am happy to hear that, but I doubt you will ever see her again."

"What do you mean, Father? What have you done?" Wallace noticed an evil look in the king's eyes, and he was suddenly afraid for his friends.

"I gave you five days and more."

"You ordered her killed!" Wallace glared at the king. "Was this all your idea, or did Saffen help you decide?"

"I make my own decisions."

"With strong influence from your adviser!"

"Whose advice I take is no concern of yours."

Wallace left the throne room and returned to his quarters to find Daniel waiting there for him. "Do you have news?" he asked.

"The prince and princess are on their way to a secret hideout. They have plenty of guards and should be safe for now," the soldier answered.

"Thank you, Daniel," Wallace stated. "You are the only one I can trust."

"I will always serve you first, Your Highness."

"No, I need you to swear loyalty to the true heir to the throne."

"Who is one and the same, My Lord."

"Lianna gave me this." Wallace unsheathed his sword and held it for Daniel to see. "This sword is to protect the true heir to the throne. This means she has foreseen that I am a protector, not an heir."

Daniel stared at the sword for a moment, then knelt before Wallace. "Whether you are a prince or a peasant, I will always serve you, My Lord, and I will do so until I die."

"Rise," the prince spoke. When the soldier stood, Wallace hugged him and said, "You are a good friend, Daniel."

"Who will you protect with this special sword?" Daniel asked.

"I do not know. Lianna said the sword will tell me."

"So, you are sworn to protect no one? That is quite odd." Daniel was puzzled.

"We must both trust the power of the sword," Wallace stated.

"I swear I will protect you and the sword, my prince!"

****

Saffen was outraged when only one of the thieves returned. He glared angrily at Drabo who looked like he had rolled all the way down the mountain. The thief's tattered clothing was caked with dirt, leaves and mud, and his body was covered with scrapes and bruises.

"You promised payment," the thief demanded.

"After the job is done!" Saffen roared. "There was no promise of payment for failure! In fact, I expect you to repay what I gave you."

"I lost that money when we were attacked. I cannot repay you."

"Who attacked you?" Saffen asked.

"It was a mountain demon that came in a whirling cloud of dust."

"You expect me to believe your men were killed by a cloud? You are a liar, Drabo!" He signaled for his guards to seize the thief.

"I am telling the truth! It was a demon!" Drabo screamed as he was dragged away.

Saffen pondered what he would tell the king. Perhaps he could blame everything on the demons and the sorcerers who lived in the mountains. That would shift the king's focus. Now that he knew what to say, Saffen hurried to confront the king.

William was sitting alone in his throne room when Saffen arrived and bowed before him. When his trusted counselor did not rise, the king became concerned. "What happened?" he asked.

"The mission failed," Saffen stated in a dramatically sad tone. He still did not rise to face the king. "Only one man survived."

"Who attacked them?"

"An evil spirit in the mountains."

"It was the wizard!" the king shouted.

"Yes, I believe it was." Saffen rose to face his king, for this was the reaction he wanted.

"Bring this wizard to me!" the king demanded.

"That will not be an easy task, Your Majesty!"

"Take as many men as you need! Take the entire army!" the king stated. "I want that wizard!"

"Yes, Your Majesty!" Saffen bowed deeply and backed out of the throne room. There was a smile on his face when he reached the grand hallway. He finally had received permission to take soldiers into the mountains to retrieve the wizard, the sorcerer. This mission would not fail!

****

Donovon walked between the rows of swordsmen who were eager to serve the true heir to the throne. Since news had spread of the prince's survival, nearly three hundred young men had eagerly volunteered to become soldiers. It was Donovon's duty to oversee their training, so he visited the encampment weekly. It was a day's ride from the fortress, but he knew Nathan and Ivan were there to protect the prince.

Donovon listened as each new soldier in turn swore to serve Prince Robert and his heirs. He touched the hilt of his sword and thought how one of these new soldiers could someday bear such a sword. Donovon felt honored that he had been chosen to lead the army, though he knew his duties kept him from his family.

Then he found himself thinking about his siblings. His two youngest brothers were among the new recruits. He had trained them well and they would be excellent soldiers. Donovon smiled proudly, knowing that his family had served the royal family for many generations, and would continue to serve the true heirs to the Farway throne.

Later that evening, Donovon greeted his brothers in the command tent. He shook their hands and patted them on their shoulders. "From this day forward, I am no longer your brother," he stated. "Now I am your commander."

"We are here to follow your orders," stated Dexter, the oldest of the two.

"We will make you proud of us," said Devon, the youngest.

"I am already proud of both of you," Donovon replied. Disregarding protocol, he hugged each of them. "Be safe."

After his brothers had left, Donovon walked alone through the encampment. As the commander, he realized that at least ten thousand more soldiers were needed before they could face King William's men. Building an army that large would take several years. And many more would die before they saw victory. A tear touched his cheek and he wiped it away with the back of his hand. Every soldier was prepared to die for the right cause, he told himself. His brothers, too, were willing die.

****

Liam followed his sister to the cave opening.

"I must go down to the village," Lianna told her brother.

"Why?" he asked. "You never go there."

"Today I must go," Lianna said.

"Then I will accompany you."

"I require no guard."

"As your brother, it is my duty to protect you," Liam argued.

"Please, I need to go alone." Lianna turned to look at her brother, who immediately stopped following her. "You need to stay in the cave."

"You have foreseen something."

"No matter what happens, do not follow me." Her eyes flashed almost in anger. "Promise!"

"I promise I will not follow." Liam moved back into the shadows of the cave and watched as his sister strolled down the mountain path toward the village. He sensed that something was wrong, but there was nothing he could do. He would not break his promise.

After an hour, Lianna reached the small town at the foot of the mountains and began looking around the marketplace. Although they rarely saw her, the village people recognized the girl from the mountains and stepped out of her way. Lianna picked up a pink silk scarf and wrapped it around her head. The merchant backed away and did not ask for payment. Lianna proceeded to the next booth, pretending not to notice several men approaching on horseback. Suddenly she was surrounded by armed soldiers.

"Come with me, witch!" the leader demanded. Two soldiers grabbed the young woman and dragged her onto a saddle, securing her hands behind her back. Lianna made no attempt to escape, but the townspeople gathered around the soldiers. One shouted, "She is not a witch!" Another pleaded, "Do not take her – she is our protector!" Ignoring the pleas, the soldiers pushed through the crowd, injuring several people as they galloped out of the town with their prisoner.

Liam watched from a nearby hill as the soldiers rode toward the castle with his sister. He wondered why she had asked him not to follow and why she had allowed the soldiers to take her. Why did she not resist? There must be a reason, he told himself. But he had promised not to interfere.

****

Robert opened the door and stepped into the hallway. There were no guards at the entrance, as Ivan had promised. No one saw the prince leave since it was early morning, and everyone was asleep. Ivan met him at the cliff with a rope to help him descend.

"I wish you were not traveling without me," Ivan said as he bid the prince farewell. "But I have obligations here."

"I understand why you must stay, and I need no one to accompany me," Robert stated. "I am an expert swordsman. I will be fine."

"Be careful, My Prince."

"I will return in two days' time," Robert promised as he grabbed the rope and slid down to a waiting boat. Three soldiers, assigned by Ivan, were waiting onboard to escort him. One of the soldiers helped the prince into the small boat and told him where to sit, so as not to capsize the vessel. The other two soldiers manned the oars.

When they reached open waters the prince and his soldiers transferred to a larger ship that carried them along the coastline and into the narrow bay leading to Creek City. Not really a city, this small town was located at the foot of the Cinaria Mountain Range. From there, the four mounted horses for their trek into the mountains.

Robert's destination was the mystical cave, where he had recovered from his wounds. Something about the cave was beckoning him to return. The summons surpassed his love for Carissa, and he could not resist it. The call of the cave grew more intense as they drew closer.

Seeing the entrance to the cave somehow made Robert feel stronger, bolder. His steps quickened as he climbed the steep path.

"Wait here," he told the soldiers when they reached the entrance. The three soldiers sat down on some boulders and only one watched as the prince disappeared into the dark cave.

The cavern appeared to be empty when Robert entered. He lifted his arms toward the high ceiling and felt soothing magic enter his body, filling him with a strength he had not felt in a long time.

"What are you doing here?" a voice spoke. Robert turned to find Liam standing near the back entrance to the spacious room.

"The cave beckoned me," the prince explained. "I had no choice but to return."

"You were told never to come back," Liam stated. "How did you find your way?"

"I followed my instincts."

Liam came closer but remained at a distance. He looked worried. "It seems the cave has had an adverse effect on you, Robert."

"The cave gives me power to survive!"

"Mysticism is no longer necessary to sustain your life," Liam explained. "You only think you need the cave. For your own sanity, you must be gone from here and never return."

"No!" the prince replied angrily. "I belong in this place! I must stay!"

"You ought to depart now." Liam slowly drew his sword.

"I am an expert swordsman and the cave will provide me the strength to defeat you." Robert drew his sword and approached Liam. Their swords struck.

"I do not want to fight you!" Liam protested as their weapons clashed again.

"I am the new master of the cave!" Robert shouted as his sword blade struck Liam in the shoulder, drawing blood.

At that moment, Donovon entered the cave, followed by Nathan. Donovon held up the sword of gold and Liam retreated.

"He attacked me!" Liam said from a distance. "I tried not to harm him."

Donovon turned to the prince. "Explain yourself."

"I … cannot," Robert replied meekly, dropping his sword to the ground and collapsing. Donovon caught the prince before his head hit the stone floor.

"It is the cave. It has confused him," Liam stated.

Suddenly the three soldiers entered the cavern and rushed at Liam, Donovon and Nathan with drawn swords. They seemed intent on reaching Robert, but Donovon stayed close to the prince.

"What is happening? Where am I?" Robert mumbled.

"Do not worry, I am here to protect you," Donovon told him. But he suddenly did not feel confident that the sword of gold would be enough to protect his prince. The power of the sword seemed to be waning, and a soldier struck the weapon, sending it flying across the room. Then the soldier's sword struck Donovon, who fell to the ground next to Robert.

In an instant, Nathan appeared and struck down the attacker. Stunned by the blow, Donovon watched as Nathan's sword glittered gold in the pale light. Why was he being protected, he wondered. Then he slipped into unconsciousness.

When he opened his eyes, Donovon saw Liam kneeling beside him. "What happened?"

"Nathan defeated the soldiers," Liam reported. "I believe they were sent to kill Robert in the cave."

"But why was Robert here?" Donovon asked. He felt a sense of pain and lifted his hand to his forehead to find it covered in blood.

"The cave called him back," Liam said.

"I do not understand."

"Besides bestowing special powers, sometimes the cave can have a negative impact on certain people," Liam state. "It can even cause some to go insane."

"Do you believe the cave had an impact on Prince Robert?" Donovon asked.

"Yes, which means he must never come here again. You will need to keep a close watch and not let him out of your sight," Liam said. "It could be deadly for him if he ever returned."

Donovon winced in pain and let out a groan. "Where is Nathan?"

"He is with Robert, waiting outside the cave. You must take them both away from here immediately."

Donovon stood up, holding his head in both hands to fight the dizziness that crept throughout his body.

"You will be fine," Liam assured him. "The cave only has a healing effect on you."

As the dizziness became manageable, Donovon took a moment to look around the large cavern. "Where is Lianna?"

"I will explain that later," Liam said. "Right now, you must return to the fortress. The princess could be in danger."

****

Liam had warned him, Donovon realized, for when he returned to the fortress the was princess gone. Ivan and some of the guards were also missing.

"Stay with the prince," Donovon told Nathan.

"I should be at your side," Nathan objected.

"I do not have time to discuss this," Donovon raised his voice. "I order you to stay with the prince!"

"Yes, sir," Nathan replied.

"I do not need you to protect me!"

"Promise me you will take your two brothers with you."

Donovon seemed annoyed but nodded. "I will, but only if I know you are with the prince."

"I will follow your orders, My Lord." Nathan watched as Donovon left the fortress with several soldiers including his two brothers.

It only took half a day for Donovon to catch up to Ivan, for the seasoned commander knew that a traitor would take the princess directly to King William. Donovon and his men quickly killed the soldiers who had betrayed them and returned Princess Carissa to the fortress.

CHAPTER 5

Plans and Misconceptions

"Is this the wizard's sister?" the king stated as he looked at the woman who had been brought before him. She had dark skin and long, black hair. Her red dress was dirty and torn. "Not so powerful now, are we?" the king laughed, then addressed Captain Worth. "Why did you bring this woman here? Your orders were to capture the wizard!"

"He will come to rescue her," Worth stated with confidence. "Liam always protects his sister."

"Is this true?" the king asked Saffen.

"Yes, he will come. Trust me," the counselor.

"He will not come," Lianna murmured softly.

"What? She speaks?" the king laughed. Then he gave the woman a cold glare. "The wizard will come, and he will trade himself for you!"

"He will not come," Lianna repeated in a slightly stronger voice.

"You cannot predict the future," Saffen stated.

"Oh, but I can!" Lianna replied as she stared directly into the king's eyes. "And you, my king, will not rule long!"

"Take her away!" the king shouted angrily.

As the soldiers pushed her out of the throne room, Lianna screamed, "You will be betrayed by the one who is closest to you! I have foreseen it!"

"Do not listen to her, My Lord," Saffen said, for he could see that the king was upset. "She is only trying to frighten you."

"She is from the mountains, so she might have knowledge of the future," the king stated. Suddenly he was calm and began to grin. He signaled for everyone to leave except his adviser. "We could use her to our advantage."

"How so, Your Majesty?" Saffen asked as he prepared to serve another brandy to the king.

"We could change her prophesies to control the people."

"That is brilliant! The people trust her. If we meet with her in private, no one else will know what she actually said!"

"Yes, and she does amuse me," the king smiled.

****

Donovon was surprised to see Liam enter the mountain fortress. He welcomed his friend with a firm handshake. "I did not expect you to visit so soon," the soldier stated. "How did you get here?"

"The details do not matter," Liam said. "We have things to discuss."

Donovon led his guest to a secluded room near the dining hall, closing the door securely. Then he turned to face Liam. "Is something wrong?"

"William has taken my sister."

"How? Why?"

"She allowed herself to be captured," Liam stated sadly.

"I do not understand. Have you talked to her?"

"I believe the soldiers were sent to capture me. They saw her in the village and took her instead. Probably they expect me to try to rescue her."

"They want you to exchange yourself for her," Donovon realized.

"She made me promise not to follow."

"You cannot go to Farway, Liam! King William wants you dead!" Donovon reminded his friend.

"I agree. But if I do not go, William will kill Lianna."

"No true king would order the execution of an innocent woman."

"You forget, Donovon. William is not the true king."

"What do you need me to do?" the swordsman asked.

"I need a few of your best men."

"Do you intend to attack Farway Castle?"

"No. I need someone to visit Glover and Ashland to secure their loyalty. You must remain with the prince. I will go to Farway alone."

"Nathan will go to Glover and Ashland. He is my second in command and can be trusted," Donovon said. "I will send two men with you to Farway where you will connect with another one of my best soldiers, Winston."

"Have you had a man at Farway all this time?" Liam did not seem surprised.

"It is always best to keep a close eye on the enemy."

"Brilliant."

"Perhaps that is what Lianna is doing?" Donovon wondered.

"No, she would have confided in me if that were the case." There was a distant look in Liam's eyes. "I can usually understand her motives, but not this time. Something is different. I am deeply concerned."

"Promise me, Liam, that you will not be captured by King William!"

"I have no choice. I must save my sister!"

"What if she foresaw that this was her destiny?" Donovon asked.

"I do not believe my sister is destined to die at the hands of an evil monarch!" Liam shouted. "I will not allow it!"

"You cannot protect her forever."

"I can, and I will! She is my sister."

"You must control your emotions, Liam, and look at the bigger picture," Donovon suggested. "Without your leadership, this kingdom will remain divided. Is that not what Lianna told us?"

"Yes, it was something like that, but I cannot remember her exact words."

"So be careful, my friend, and do not fall into a trap."

"I will remember your words, Donovon, and I will return," Liam promised.

****

Wallace was too angry to face his father. Instead, he headed directly to his quarters with Daniel following him.

"I am sorry, Your Highness. I did not know about this," Daniel said as they entered the privacy of the prince's quarters. "I surely would have warned you."

"I know my father. He has no intentions of letting her leave here alive. No prisoner ever leaves this castle alive!" Wallace angrily slammed his fist upon the large wooden table that stood in the middle of the room. "How did the soldiers find her?"

"I heard she was in the village marketplace."

"Lianna never goes there!" Wallace began pacing nervously around the room.

"It is not your fault, My Lord!"

"I should have been there to protect her!"

"There must be something you can do to help her," Daniel suggested.

"If I visit her, my father will think me a traitor."

"That would be risky."

"We need a plan!" Wallace walked over to the largest window in the room. He was silent for several minutes before saying, "I could offer to be my father's liaison. I could convince him that I understand the mysticism of the mountain regions. That would at least give me a chance to talk to her."

"It might work."

"We will make it work!" Wallace said. "First, fetch me some books on this mysticism or anything related to it. I must make myself more knowledgeable than Saffen."

"Yes, Your Highness."

When Daniel left, Wallace knelt by the window and held his head in his hands. He felt like crying, but no tears came.

****

Prince Robert was sitting alone at a table reading in his quarters when Donovon entered and bowed. The prince immediately ordered him to rise and then sit beside him.

"I wish I could show you the new recruits, my prince," Donovon stated. "You would be so proud."

"I heard that your two youngest brothers are among them," Robert said.

"Yes, they are eager to serve the rightful heir to the throne."

"I am honored to have them." The prince diverted his focus from Donovon and toward a distant corner of the room.

"Is something wrong, Your Highness?" Donovon asked. "You seem worried."

"Do you realize it may be a long time before we regain the throne?"

"I am aware that it will take many years to rebuild an army."

"My uncle has already killed most of my family members and continues to hunt for more." The prince rose from his chair and walked to the end of the table. "I cannot hide forever."

"We are soldiers, you and I, and hiding is not something we do well," Donovon responded. "I promise you, Robert, it will not be much longer. Soon we will have enough men to protect you wherever you wish to reside."

"That is good news, Donovon, and it gives us hope," the prince stated. "But I fear we may be in this fortress for a very long time. Maybe forever."

"I have given you my promise that it will not be forever, My Prince."

Robert smiled at the soldier, though he did not quite believe his words. "I will hold you to that promise, Donovon. But forever may come sooner than we expect."

****

King William looked skeptically at his son. "When did you learn about the mountain region and its religion?" he asked.

"I have studied many things, Father, and I have retained much knowledge," Wallace replied. "The mountains are part of our kingdom and I thought their religious beliefs and mysticism should be studied."

"Do you not think it odd that the people who reside there believe in wizards and magic?"

"Few visit the region, so I would expect the mountain residents to hold onto their ancient beliefs."

"Do you really think you can communicate with this witch woman?"

"Her people may see her as a witch, but she is entirely human," Wallace stated. "I assure you, Father, I know how to convince her that I believe she has special powers. I know all of the terminology."

"Fine. But I only need you to convince her to be civil with her king and to treat me with respect," King William said. "I would like to meet privately with her tomorrow morning to hear more about her visions for the future."

"Being your liaison would be my pleasure!" Wallace bowed slightly before leaving the throne room. He glanced briefly at Saffen, who had listened to the entire conversation. Then Wallace retired to his quarters, knowing it would not be good if he seemed too eager to visit Lianna.

An hour later, Wallace stepped into the room where Lianna was confined. He dismissed the inside guard and slowly approached the woman who huddled trembling by the fireside. She looked up and saw him but did not move. He reached for her hand and lifted her toward him.

"I was afraid you would not come," she whispered as they kissed.

"I convinced my father to assign me as your liaison," Wallace explained.

"How did you do that?"

"I told him I knew everything about the ancient mountain region and its religion."

She laughed. "You?"

"Hey, I can be quite convincing when I want something."

"But our religion is the same as the rest of the country," Lianna stated. "The only thing ancient is the powers within the cave."

"I know. But my father has no clue. And he allowed me to see you."

"If only we had more time!"

"What does that mean? Do you believe you are in danger?"

"No, I am safe now that you are with me, Wallace. How long can you stay?"

"I think it might take about an hour to convince you to be nice when you visit the king tomorrow. I wish it would take all night, but that might arouse suspicion."

"An hour will be sufficient, my love!" she whispered.

✶✶✶✶✶✶✶✶✶✶✶✶✶✶✶✶✶✶✶✶✶

Draped in a dark cloak, Liam stood alone outside the castle wall gazing intently at the nearest of the four towers. From his informants, he had heard that his sister was imprisoned in the northwest tower. At least she was not in the dungeon and probably was not being tortured, he told himself.

Liam knew it was a trap. Capturing Lianna was the king's way of getting him to the castle. Well, it had worked. He was at the castle.

A rider approached and Liam pulled his cloak closer to his head so as not to be detected. He relaxed when he saw it was one of the two men who had traveled from the mountains with him.

"Yo, Bradley! Do you have news?" Liam asked.

"She is in the northwest tower in the upper room," Bradley reported. "The king knows that she has the wisdom to foresee the future and he plans to use her gift to his advantage."

"How did he hear about her power?"

"From what I could tell, she made a prediction about the king, but I do not know what it was."

"That was a mistake!" Liam sighed. "Hopefully she does not fall for any more of the king's tricks!"

"Pardon me for saying this, sir, but it may all be part of Lianna's plan."

"If getting captured and revealing everything to the king is her plan, then I am not sticking around here for moral support. She is on her own." Liam signaled for his horse, which was brought to him. He mounted the brown steed and turned it away from the castle.

"We cannot leave her alone here!"

"We can, and we will. There is no reason for us to stay. I have other places to go and better things to do." Liam spurred the horse into a gallop and headed toward the mountains. His two men followed.

CHAPTER 6

Swordsmanship and Mysticism

Prince Robert and Princess Carissa greeted Donovon as he entered their private chambers. Although he was in command of the fortress, Donovon seldom spoke to the princess. He respected her privacy and politely expressed his gratitude for being invited to dine with the royal couple.

"I apologize for not inviting you sooner, General," the prince stated. "I had assumed you wanted to be with your family."

"Are they well?" the princess asked.

"Yes, they are well," Donovon replied. "Thank you so much for asking." He sat in the chair next to the prince. The princess sat on the other side of her husband.

"Is Nathan in charge of security tonight?" the prince asked. A servant poured and tested the wine while another set a bowl of fruit on the table.

"No, Liam needed him to travel to Glover and Ashland," the soldier answered. "We need to secure our alliances." Donovon waited to drink his wine until after the prince took a sip.

"I know we can count on the support of the regents in the both areas," the prince stated. "But did you need to send Nathan?"

"He is very good at negotiating and is loyal to you, My Prince."

"I only feel secure when you or Nathan are near," Robert stated.

"Your Highness, all of the soldiers have sworn allegiance to you."

"That does not mean they cannot be bribed. You have no clue how far my uncle will go to see me dead!"

"You forget, My Prince, that I have seen his evil first-hand. He also murdered my father and two of my brothers!"

"Yes, I did forget, and you must forgive me, Sir Donovon."

Two servants filled the table with food, tested it, then promptly left the room. Donovon began to eat after the royal couple had taken their first bites.

"Is something wrong, Your Highness?" Donovon asked the prince. "You seem rather nervous tonight."

"At times it seems like the guards are not standing outside our door," Robert replied. "Like now."

By his expression, Donovon could tell that the prince truly believed that the guards were no longer at the door. He excused himself from the table, quietly stood up and walked slowly to the door. When he opened it, five strangers barged into the room with swords drawn. "Guards!" Donovon called for reinforcements as he grabbed his sword and moved closer to the prince.

"Protect Carissa!" the prince ordered. He drew his own sword and began fighting the intruders.

"This sword protects only you!" Donovon shouted. That is when he noticed that his sword of gold was guiding him towards the princess. Instantly, fifteen guards rushed into the room and took over the fight. Donovon guided the princess into the next room, then went back for the prince, who was continuing to fight the intruders.

"Is the princess safe?" Robert asked, and Donovon nodded.

"Come, Your Highness," the swordsman said. "Let the guards handle this." He gently pushed Prince Robert through the doorway and into the room where Carissa waited. The royal couple immediately embraced, and the prince continued to hold his wife close. Donovon closed the door and stood near it.

"We are no longer safe here!" Robert shouted. "We must leave at once!"

"No, we must remain a while longer," Donovon replied. "You cannot leave this fortress without Liam's permission."

"Liam cannot give me orders!"

"All of us take orders from Liam!" Donovon explained. "You forget, without him you would be dead."

"But why must I remain here? I do not understand."

"We cannot risk you being drawn to the cave again, Your Highness. Being there had an adverse effect on you."

"I feel fine."

"Visiting the cave again could cause you to go insane. We cannot take that chance."

****

King William looked up as Lianna entered the throne room accompanied by two guards. Her hands were tied securely to a rope at her waist. "Leave us," the king commanded. Soon he was alone in the enormous hall with the woman. For several minutes, the king only looked at her and did not speak.

"You summoned me," Lianna spoke without raising her head to look at the king.

"You still refuse to acknowledge me as king? This defiance grows tiresome." William stood up from his throne and walked down the steps toward the woman. "I know your weakness, Lianna. You only speak the truth."

As he stepped closer, the woman raised her head and looked at him. Her dark eyes were filled with hate. "You are not my king!"

"Careful. Do not talk nasty to me or you will be punished. A mere woman like you would never survive my torture chamber," he threatened with an evil grin.

"I know you will not kill me."

"True. I need you."

"You need my gift, you tyrant!"

"That gift could prove quite useful to me. Do not forget that I wear the crown and King Anthony is dead," the king sneered.

"Dead only because you murdered him!" Lianna took a step back.

"So, tell me, Lianna, why do my people hate me?"

"I just told you!"

"Did you foresee that I would be king?"

Lianna turned her eyes downward before answering meekly, "Yes."

"And where did you get this notion that I will not rule much longer? Tell me!"

"I cannot control what I foresee."

"Who did you say will betray me?"

"Someone close." With those words, the woman sank to her knees.

"Who? Tell me who!" The king grabbed Lianna by her hair and raised her face until she was looking directly into his eyes.

"Evil! All I see is evil!" she screamed like a mad person. Then suddenly she was calm, and her voice was weak. "Nothing. Nothing else."

"Useless! Your information is useless!" The king grabbed a handful of the woman's hair and pulled until she fell sobbing to the ground. "Be gone!" the king shouted. "Guards!"

Two guards entered and dragged Lianna out of the room.

Saffen stepped out from behind the throne. "Why do you let her live?" the king's counselor asked.

"Her insights have been quite useful and perhaps she will benefit me again," the king replied. "Besides, she amuses me. Such defiance!"

"I am glad that something amuses you, My King," Saffen said. "But she revealed no secrets."

"True. She stated nothing new, but that is not what the people will hear," King William stated. "You and I will control what the people hear."

Saffen smiled, then proceeded to tell the king what prophesies he thought the people should hear.

****

The sword of gold was laying on the table in front of Donovon. He reached for it, then backed away. Something was different. The sword no longer beckoned him to protect Prince Robert. This confused him, for he had sworn to protect the true heir to the throne. Donovon touched the golden hilt with his fingertips and the entire sword glimmered gold. What did this mean, he wondered? Gingerly he picked up the sword, slid it into its sheath and left the room.

After the attack, Donovon ordered security increased throughout the castle. Guards found responsible for the infiltration had been disciplined and dismissed. No matter how much he tightened security, Donovon still worried about the safety of the prince and spent hours near the royal suite. Today was no different. Instead of visiting his family, he planned to spend the day with Prince Robert. Upon entering the royal suite, he found the prince sitting alone in the reception area.

"Where is Princess Carissa?" Donovon asked.

"She is resting," Prince Robert replied.

"Is someone near her?"

"The guards are outside her chamber door. Why are you so concerned?"

"Why are you so calm, Your Highness?" Donovon asked. "It has only been three days since the attack. I am concerned that it might happen again."

"When I asked that we leave, you assured me that we would be safer here. We must trust you."

"So, you are no longer worried?"

"I would know if we were in danger."

For a moment, Donovon was confused. Then he remembered that Robert had spent many weeks in the cave. Perhaps he had gained the power to foresee the future, much like Lianna's gift. Or maybe he could sense something was amiss?

"I plan to stay very near, so please let me know if there is any danger lurking," Donovon stated. He touched the top of his sword as he walked across the room and sat in a chair close to the chamber door.

"You will be the first to know," the prince stated.

Donovon relaxed in the cushioned chair and struggled to keep his eyes open. He was awakened by the sound of Robert's voice.

"Are you not worried that I may try to escape?"

"Uh? Sorry. Guess I dozed off for a moment," Donovon apologized.

"Perhaps you should take a break?" the prince suggested. "I promise I will not escape until tomorrow."

"You are not a prisoner here."

"This seems very much like a prison to me, Donovon."

"We are only trying to protect you from your enemies and from yourself."

"Well, this protection grows tiresome!"

"I understand, but it is necessary. Do you not agree?"

"Yes, but that does not mean I like it."

****

King William stared at his counselor in disbelief.

"How did Prince Robert survive?" he asked. "There were no survivors!"

"I do not know how it happened," Saffen stated. "But the fact remains that he is alive and is with Princess Carissa."

William rose from the throne and looked around the empty room. "I am glad you told me in private, Saffen. We would not want everyone to know about this. Now, what do we do about the situation?"

"I already staged an assassination attempt, but it failed."

"Really, Saffen, you should leave this type of thing to the military!" the expressed his displeasure. "Your last two plots have failed!"

"We came close this time, Your Majesty. The attack force was in the same room as the prince and princess."

"Then what went wrong? Why did they fail to kill the prince?"

"They had an unexpected guest at the dinner – Sir Donovon."

"Donovon? That traitor!" the king roared. "We must put him at the top of our hit list!"

"And Liam has still not come to rescue his sister."

"Another one of your failed ideas, Saffen."

"But the false prophesy idea will work," the counselor assured his king. "I am most certain!"

"Yes, it was a brilliant idea to announce that the outer regions plan to send their armies to help us. That will scare those who oppose me!"

"And everybody believes it was foreseen by Lianna!" Saffen smiled. "You were right, Your Majesty. She will be quite useful."

"I only hope I can control my temper when I am in her presence," King William said. "She has spoken rudely to me. One of these times I may order her to be executed."

"That would be most unfortunate."

"But then again, who would know that she was dead? Only you and me."

"Brilliant strategy, My King, brilliant strategy!"

"Would you pour me another brandy?" the king asked.

"Yes, Your Majesty," Saffen smiled. "With pleasure!"

Saffen bowed deeply before backing out of the throne room. His plans had worked perfectly, and the king was doing everything he suggested with the help of the proper concoctions. Now if he could just eliminate his rival and the evil witch, he would be in complete control of the insane king.

CHAPTER 7

Loyalties and Lies

Daniel waited patiently for Wallace to react to the news he had brought. The prince only continued to look out the nearby window.

"Your Highness?" Daniel spoke after several minutes. "Do you not find this news alarming?"

Finally, Wallace turned to face his friend. "It does not surprise me that the king has twisted her words. It was expected."

"What can we do about it?"

"Nothing. We can only hope that the people will not believe the lie."

"We must get Lianna out of here!"

"I cannot do anything yet," Wallace replied sadly.

"Why are we waiting?"

"She asked me to wait."

"I do not understand. What if the king orders her to be executed?"

"Lianna must have a reason for asking me to wait," Wallace stated.

"Nothing could be worth risking her life!"

Wallace nodded, then was silent for several minutes before hurrying out of the room in the direction of the king's quarters. Daniel followed, but stayed several steps behind.

King William had been eating his supper alone and was surprised to see his son enter the royal quarters unannounced. The king signaled for Wallace to join him at the large table, but the prince remained standing. "I only need a moment," he told his father.

"Is something troubling you?" the king asked in a concerned tone. He had never seen his son look so worried.

"What do you intend to do with Lianna?" Wallace asked, staring directly into his father's eyes.

The king looked puzzled. "Why would this concern you, my son?"

"Would you sentence an innocent woman to death, Father?" Wallace asked. "Would you be that callous? Could you really do something that evil?"

The king pushed his dinner plate away and turned his entire focus toward his son. "Why does this affect you?"

"Every decision you make affects me! I am your son, your heir!"

"You assume you are my heir." The king took a swallow of wine and, moving his dinner plate towards him, resumed eating. "But this is my kingdom, not yours, and these are my decisions, not yours."

Wallace was infuriated by the king's nonchalant tone. He clenched his fists and tried to control his anger, but his face betrayed him by turning slightly red. He hoped the king would not notice.

After taking several bites of food, the king looked up at his son. "Does this witch woman really mean that much to you?"

"She means nothing to me."

The king stood up, strode over to his son and began to walk slowly around him. "I think she means everything to you." The king stopped in front of Wallace. "And I think Saffen was totally right about you ... again."

The prince took a deep breath and regained his composure. "You have not answered my first question."

"What I do with Lianna is my own decision. I may just execute her to annoy you!" The king clapped his hands loudly and five guards entered the room, followed by Saffen. "Leave me now!"

Wallace left the room only to find Daniel waiting for him outside the door. With one look, the prince could tell that Daniel had heard the entire conversation. "I should have listened to you, Daniel. We must get Lianna out of here tonight!" Wallace told his friend as they hurried toward the northwest tower. "It might already be too late!"

They rushed into Lianna's room and found her crying. Wallace embraced her and wiped away the tears on her cheeks. Daniel waited by the door.

"I thought I would never see you again," Lianna said.

"Have you foreseen something?" Wallace asked.

"There is no future for us!" she sobbed.

"What did you foresee?"

"It is too horrible!"

"I am getting you out of here right now!" Wallace promised.

"We will never escape together!" she warned as he led her out the door with Daniel right behind them.

"We can escape, and we will be together!" the prince assured her. "We will be safe as soon as we get to the main hall. There is a secret exit."

"The hall should be empty at this time of night," Daniel stated.

"Passing through the throne room could be a problem," Wallace noted. "My father likes to sit on the throne."

"Is there another way?" Lianna asked.

Wallace shook his head. "No, the secret passageway begins right outside the throne room in case there is danger and the king is required to escape."

Wallace held Lianna's hand as they walked down a long corridor. Suddenly five guards appeared, and Daniel immediately attacked them. Wallace drew his sword and left Lianna's side to assist Daniel, but felt a strange sensation creeping up the arm that held his sword. Looking down, he saw the sword glowing and almost pulling him in the other direction. He stopped as he realized the sword was telling him to go back to Lianna to protect her.

Lianna also seemed surprised when Wallace came back to her instead of running forward to attack the guards. He stayed by her side and waited for the guards to come near her before he fought them. Two of them got past Daniel, only to be quickly defeated by Wallace.

When all five guards were laying on the ground severely wounded or dead, Lianna looked up at Wallace. "What happened?" she asked.

"It was the sword," the prince explained. "You are the one I must protect."

"No," she replied. "Why?"

Daniel came toward them. "Obviously you are an heir to the throne," he stated.

"I cannot be an heir," Lianna said. "I am not of royal blood."

"Perhaps it is your child," Daniel speculated.

"Are you pregnant?" Wallace asked. There was a concerned look in his eyes.

Lianna looked at Wallace and answered, "Yes."

"All the more reason for us to get her out of here!" Daniel said. This time he led the way down the staircase, through another long corridor and toward the main hall.

****

Liam slipped into the darkness of the castle corridor, sword in hand. He was alone and therefore risking only his life. He knew every passageway, having spent many years serving the royal family.

Within minutes he reached his destination undetected. He grabbed the latch and opened the door slowly. The room was empty. Maybe he was too late, Liam thought to himself.

He quietly closed the door and headed for the main area of the castle. The feeling of doom grew stronger and his heart beat faster. He no longer worried about being detected by the castle guards. His only concern was for the safety of his sister.

****

Saffen smiled at King William. "So, you finally understand what I have been telling you. We cannot trust Wallace."

"He seemed very concerned for our prisoner," the king stated. "That worries me."

The two were alone in the throne room, with the king sitting stately on his throne. It was his favorite place to sit, especially when he felt too weak to walk to his chambers. Lately he had felt dizzy.

"Do you desire another brandy?" Saffen asked.

"No more today," William answered. "Perhaps some water."

Saffen smiled. It was just as easy to hide the poisoned drops in water.

"Thank you," the king said as he accepted the drink.

Saffen moved closer. "I know he has been with her, but I had no proof until recently," he told the king. "My guards reported that he has spent much time visiting her and they even suspect they spend most nights together."

"She is but a commoner," King William frowned. "Why would he be interested in her?"

"Lianna is a very beautiful and crafty woman."

"She has bewitched him, I am sure," the king determined.

"With her mystical powers."

"All the more reason to put an end to this!"

"What are you saying, Your Majesty?"

"Execute her first thing in the morning!"

"Why wait until morning?" Saffen stepped back after he spoke, hoping he had not sounded too anxious to end the woman's life. Then another idea came into his head. "I could make it look like she took her own life."

The king spent a few minutes deep in thought before answering, "Yes, that could work." He stroked his shaggy long beard and looked off into the distance. "Better yet ..."

"Yes?" Saffen waited for the king's next words.

"We could make it look like she was killed trying to assassinate me."

"Excellent!"

"But that might make her look like a martyr." The king had second thoughts about his idea.

"We will make it look like she is just a crazy person." Saffen continued to speculate.

"Quiet!" the king ordered. "Do you hear something?"

Saffen listened but heard nothing. "Maybe you imagined it?"

"There is someone coming."

"How odd. Perhaps we should hide?"

"Turn down the lights," the king stated. "I will remain sitting on the throne where I belong."

Saffen blew out a few candles and slipped behind the throne as someone entered the room from a side door. Three people began to walk across the darkened room.

"Going somewhere?" King William asked as they passed in front of his throne.

Wallace froze when he heard his father's voice. He quickly stepped in front of Lianna and Daniel. "Father!"

King William stepped down from his throne and walked up to his son. "Look, Saffen! It appears my son is attempting to free a dangerous prisoner," the king sneered. "That is the ultimate betrayal."

"Guards!" the king called.

No guards responded to the king's call for help, but Saffen stepped out from behind the throne, armed with a small knife.

"Father!" Wallace noticed a glazed look in the king's eyes. "Is something wrong?" He moved closer to his father as the man seemed to stagger.

"I trusted you!" the king shouted as he pulled out a dagger and stabbed his own son.

"You never trusted me!" Wallace said as he fell to the ground, fatally wounded. "I … have never … betrayed you."

"You are a monster! You murdered your own son!" Lianna screamed as she rushed at the king, beating him with her fists. "He never would have betrayed you!"

Daniel pulled the woman away from the king and they both bent down by Wallace, who was mumbling something with his dying breath. "Take the sword, Daniel," they could hear him saying. "Protect them!"

Daniel reached for the sword of gold.

Then the prince died.

"What have I done?" The king stumbled backwards until he fell on the steps leading to the throne. Seeing his son die seemed to shock the king back to reality. For the first time in years his head felt no confusion, no craziness. "What have I done?"

"Most unfortunate." Saffen noticed William was slipping back to normal and soon would be out of his control. He knew he needed to act quickly. "It appears you killed the prince … and then … your son killed you!" Saffen said as he drove a dagger into the king's heart.

"You! You are the one she said … would betray me!" The king slumped over, dead.

"We must leave!" Daniel told Lianna as he dragged her away from Wallace.

"No!" she protested, but her grief weakened her. It was a struggle, but Daniel was able to get the woman out of the throne room and safely into the main hall. A soldier was standing near the door. Daniel raised his sword, but the soldier made no move toward them.

"I am Winston, one of Donovon's men. I am here to help," the soldier spoke.

At that moment, a dozen soldiers rushed into the room. Lianna sank to the floor as Daniel raised the sword of gold to defend her. There were too many soldiers for him to fight, even with Winston's help. And more castle guards were rapidly approaching.

Suddenly Liam was there, fighting alongside Winston and Daniel. "Get her out of here!" Liam shouted at Daniel, for he noticed who held the special sword. "We will hold them off."

The authoritative tone of Liam's voice convinced Daniel to obey orders. He sheathed his sword, lifted Lianna up into his arms and carried her through the doorway that led to the secret passageway. He had only gone a few feet when he heard Liam and Winston following them. "What about the soldiers?" Daniel asked, doubting that victory had come so swiftly.

"We took care of them," Winston assured him. "Keep moving!"

Liam silently led the other three out of the castle where horses were waiting for them. Lianna finally seemed to notice her brother and began to weep. "They killed Wallace!" she cried, clinging to Liam.

"I know. It is my fault for not coming sooner," Liam answered. "Right now, we must get you to safety!"

The four quietly slipped into the darkness.

The soldiers did not follow, because, according to legend, a mysterious wall blocked them inside the throne room, and they were immobilized.

Liam felt a heavy sadness as he led the way to the mountain cave. He knew the evil Counselor Saffen would claim the crown, but that was not what concerned him the most.

His sister was safe, and that was all that mattered

ABOUT THE AUTHOR

Heir to the Magic

BY TERRI ELLEN MYHRA

My sister Jane is extremely meticulous about exactly where she places and puts things, and I think the same is true for her with words and how she writes. On the farm growing up she really cared a lot about her barn boots that she wore daily to do the chores. I recall once when I couldn't find my own barn boots to wear to go out and do the chores, and when my sister discovered that I had hers on she got quite mad at me, to put it lightly.

Another time I remember going into her room and taking one of her shirts. She didn't like that either, but at the time I didn't quite get why. Years later I of course understand how annoying little sisters can probably be.

She one time wanted my daughter to put the newspaper in a certain spot unbeknownst to her and let Tara know exactly where she wanted it to go. So, the same goes for her way with words. Jane instinctively knows where they belong and what they should say. I love her use of dialogue in this prequel and how well everything flows together so naturally.

It was years ago, but we were already adults when my sister Jane and I mounted our elaborately decorated horses on the merry-go-round at one of the local fairs. We didn't care that we were well beyond the age we should have been to have ridden such a contraption. We did what we wanted to do, and we have no regrets.

When I was seven years old, I had a choice to go with my mom to a Republican convention or go with my sister Jane to spend the day at the carnival where she babysat some kids for our neighbors who ran a carnival outfit. It didn't take me long to decide to go with Jane. What seven-year-old wouldn't want free rides and a day of amusement and cotton candy? So, I spent the day with Jane and I never looked back. Ever.

Pretty Freaky or Freak Me Out

It was in the decade of the 1970s, eons ago, you might say. Jane was the one who conned me into going on the double ferris wheel at the Wisconsin State Fair and who also somehow, although upon reflection, I have no idea how she managed it, convinced me to partake in a roller coaster ride with her. Now this wasn't just any roller coaster. No, it wasn't the kind for kids or one that was just mediocre. It was a real, downright scary one, a real thriller, although I surely didn't think so at the time. She also manipulated me into going to the haunted mansion at the fair that was equipped with live characters dressed up as ghosts and monsters who jumped out and scared us.

We always showed our Guernsey cows at the Wisconsin State Fair every year. We stayed there for a week, so there was plenty of time to do fun things like walk our cows down the midway and let them drink out of the 'bubbler,' better known to most as the water fountain. Other times we would check out the freak animals and even the freak people on display on the midway.

My sisters Jane and Judy always wanted to go on the Super Himalaya, a ride that went fast at supersonic speeds while simultaneously playing the latest seventies disco music of the day. The bright lights of this ride gleamed and shimmered as it rotated at warp speed for all who dared go on it. Once it completed its rotation the ride switched and went just as fast if not faster in a backward direction. I have to say that the part that my sisters and I liked best was when everyone got off the ride and immediately got back on again to get a free ride.

I remember the barker at the freak show shouted these words to passersby as I stood next to my sister Jane in wonder looking at the oddities portrayed on the larger-than-life sized canvases depicting Frogman, Rubber Lady, the Siamese twins, Monkey Woman and the like. "Step right up! Get your tickets. Dare to come inside. What you are about to see will make women faint and men cry."

Outside the exhibit the amusement show announcer

parroted his eclectic calls, enticing us to spend our last dollars on what could be found inside, something, he said, that was so disturbing, so shocking that we would be astonished and mortified, and it would make us scream and run out in panic. The sideshow employee made us feel somehow special that we would be the ones lucky enough to feast our eyes on the show's enchanting acts. In addition, we were further persuaded to go inside because the woman next to the barker had a giant cobra slithering around her neck, and after that 'Popeye,' the man who could literally pop his eyes out of their sockets both at one time, showed us his talents.

I often look back and contemplate those long-gone days of our youth in that by-gone era of the previous century. I now wonder what I would have done if my sister Jane hadn't tempted and dared me to do some of those things like going on decadent amusement rides or seeing the freaks at the freak show. How dull my life would have been if I would have missed out on those thrilling tidbits of entertainment. Then, too, I think about how different things would be now if I never had the chance to see Jane's written work as I saw it as a child, or even as I see how it has evolved today. I sure know that I wouldn't be writing this right now. All in all, I would have really missed out and my entire life would have been drastically altered.

The roller coasters we ride in life are the ones that we don't want to miss. Those are the thrills that make life worth living. The twists and turns, the ups and downs are where we learn. The smooth path is never a lesson. Jane was my roller coaster and she sure brought the thrills.

It has become increasingly evident that my sister has

much more energy than I will ever have. She has always been this way, too. She has constantly had many projects in the works, so I really shouldn't have been too surprised when she informed me that she had completed her prequel, her second novel in the *Sword of Gold* series. This novel really excited me because it was so interesting and thought-provoking. The characters came alive and left me wanting more when the tale subsided. Her writing has a way of always doing that sort of thing for me, so that, too, came as no shock.

The ups and downs and adventures of the characters in *Heir to the Throne* provided me with thrills and definitely left me wanting more. I craved another ticket, another ride. I was willing to pay more for what was hidden behind that shrouded curtain of her pages and wanted to go back into the past, whether it was that of my own childhood of the 1960s and '70s, or the medieval ages exemplified in this novel. I needed to know more about the sword of gold and its magic and secrets.

Touch of Gold

My sister Jane served as a sort of mentor for me as I wanted to be like her and replicate her creations. So, she really inspired me with her menagerie of talents in writing, drawing and creativity. She always has and continues to do so. I always tried to emulate Jane.

Jane took me to a concert and brought music and magic back into my life. She has a plethora of talents and should spend her days writing. She is that good.

In the olden days Jane had a Barbie doll named Jeanne. She was blonde, just like Jane. Her other doll was Louise and she, too, was blonde. She had short hair and Jeanne wore her hair up in a ponytail secured at the top of her head. Each of my sisters got a doll that mirrored their hair color when we went to Milwaukee to see my grandmother who was sick at Saint Luke's hospital. We had to wait in the car because some of us were too young to go in and I think my mom thought the dolls might distract and give us something to occupy our time as we waited for her at the hospital. My doll had dark hair like me, and I wanted my doll to look like Jane's dolls and be blonde instead.

Often, we would play kings and queens with these dolls, devising our own little pretend fairy world rooted in our creative imaginations, imaginations that would one day evolve into the creativity seen in Jane's writing abilities portrayed in the story that follows. It is my contention that these things, these experiences helped give my sister her Midas touch for the written word.

Sisters and Such

Currently Jane writes books about sisters and protecting them, and that thought never ceases to remind me of the way she protected me and took me under her wing when I was a child.

Now, back to that freak show that Jane forced me to see with her. I was terrified to go in and I remember it cost a dollar, and in those days, we thought that was outrageously expensive. Well, it really was a lot of money for the time, especially for farm girls.

When we entered the tan canvased tent that resembled a circus, we immediately saw a fat lady and then a bearded lady. Then we saw all the other freaks on exhibit, and we were surprised that we were even able to talk to them. After a while the barker called all the spectators together and told us that he had something that was so horrible, so grotesque, that we would go into shock. He went on to describe an alligator man who had scales covering his entire body. The catch was that you had to pay yet another dollar to see that sideshow, but the man assured us that seeing the man hidden behind the curtain would be well worth it. Well readers, I want you to know that like that alligator man, my sister's book is well worth it.

Well, the freaks are gone now forever, and are never coming back. You will be hard-pressed to find anything close to what the sideshows offered this side of Coney Island. Seeing freaks became unethical shortly after our encounter with them. The freak shows were shut down, never to return. Little did we all know then how drastically our world would change with a politically correct society and the death of innocence. Today we have seen circuses become obsolete due to alleged improper treatment of elephants and other animals trained to please and entertain the public. Like the sideshow freaks the past consisted of a time when no one questioned or thought of the idea that these acts were abusive.

Gone too are the knights and the age of chivalry, their swords, castles and moats with them, just like the freaks. Gone are the damsels in distress, and they won't be back, but you can still find them in books like this. Here, enthroned within the written word, the bygone era remains for ever encased with all its thrills and magic, all for your enjoyment.

It is with my great honor that I present to you Jane's second novel in the *Sword of Gold* series, *Heir to the Throne*. I only hope that you find it as entrancing as I do. So, step right up and enjoy my sister's kaleidoscope of twists and turns that is inherent in what she does so well. Here is her magical story of kings and castles, a tale that embodies her gift with literature and everything she writes. Immerse yourself into a story that Jane weaves so well, one that has been spun so finely into gold.

The Glistening Sword

BY TERRI ELLEN MYHRA

Magical swords and caves enchanted,

Ladies and lords,

Wishes granted

Faraway abodes, mystical places

Sword is gold, Hidden embraces,

Throne not known

Everything regal,

Hidden, not shown,

Nothing is legal

Now listen

About a sword that glistens,

Glover, Farway,

Mountains of magic

Do things our way

Something tragic

To the castle

What a hassle

Secure the palace

Evil and malice

Royal charmer

Loyal, don't harm her

In his armor

Princess

Must confess,

regal dress,

Her highness

Blood stain

On his reign

King insane

Have to wince,

Save the prince

A king evil,

Total upheaval,

Throne retrieval

Before it's over

Faraway and Glover

Sisters, stitches,

Blisters and witches

Horses prancing,

almost dancing

Even romancing

Sometimes enhancing,

Backwards glancing

Lances lancing

Weapons protecting,

Royalty expecting

Problems detecting

Often neglecting

Mystical cave

Knight and knave

Kings parading,

Foes invading

Secrets cascading,

Masquerading

Horses and steeds

Evil and greed

Warnings to heed.

Where is my king,

My Lord?

Where is my sword?

Story's told

Will unfold,

Crown bestowed,

Sword of gold.

The Island of Farway

Kingdom of Ashland

Kingdom of Glover

Kingdom of Farway

Made in the USA
Middletown, DE
27 May 2021